Lynn Arnason

About Starters Stories

This new range of books offers a stimulating selection of fiction for young readers to tackle themselves. The language is graded into three reading levels – red, blue, and green. The stories are accompanied by colorful and lively illustrations.

The topic dealt with in each STORY is expanded upon in an accompanying STARTERS FACTS book, which provides a valuable source of information and topic-based activities.

In this case the story **The Dinosaur's Footprint** is matched by an informative FACTS book called **Dinosaurs.**

Reading Consultants

Betty Root, Tutor-in-charge, Center for the Teaching of Reading, University of Reading.

Geoffrey Ivimey, Senior Lecturer in Child Development, University of London Institute of Education.

The Dinosaur's Footprint

by
Richard Blythe

illustrated by
Sandy Connor

Starters Stories • Blue 3

'Let's go and look at the
big yellow monsters,' said Kate.
'Oh, yes!' said her brother.
His name was Simon.
'I love listening to the noise
the monsters make,' said Kate.

Simon and Kate set off
on their bikes.
They rode up a steep hill.
When they were nearly at the top,
Kate said, 'Listen!
I can hear the monsters!'

From the top of the hill
they looked down into a valley.
Some men were making a new road.
They were using big yellow machines.
The machines were nearly
as big as houses.

'Look at the yellow monsters,' said Simon.
'Come on!' shouted Kate.
They rode down the hill.
The machines were shoving the earth
to make the new road.

The machines growled and roared.
They made dark clouds of dust.
Some had wheels bigger than a man.
Some had tracks like tanks.

'Hello,' said the man in charge.
'Have you come to watch?'
'Yes,' said Kate.
'We like watching your machines.'
'They're a bit like dinosaurs,' said Simon.
The man smiled. 'Stand here,' he said,
'and you will be safe.'

Just then a large machine rolled by.
The driver waved to the children.
The machine scraped up a heap of earth.
It growled and groaned as it
pushed against the earth.

When the machine had gone
you could see the rock which
had been underneath the earth.
Kate was looking at the rock,
which had just been scraped clean.
'Look!' she cried. 'A footprint!'

Kate pointed to the rock.
There was a big mark on it.
The mark was nearly a yard long.
'It is a footprint!' cried Simon.

'Let's have a look,' said Kate.
'It might be a dinosaur's footprint.'
The man in charge led the way.
'What a surprise!' he said.

They all bent over the rock.
'Look, claw marks,' said Simon.
'It is a dinosaur's footprint,' said Kate.
'Yes, it could be,' said the man.
'This rock is very, very old.'

'How old is it?' asked Simon.
The man had to think.
'More than a hundred million
years,' he said.
'Were dinosaurs alive then?'
asked Simon.

'Yes,' said Kate, 'they were.
We learned about them at school.
This rock was mud then.
Since then it has turned into stone.'

'So a footprint in mud,' said Simon,
'has turned into a footprint in stone!'
'Goodness!' said the man.
'I wonder what sort of dinosaur it was?'
'We must try and find out,' said Kate.

The man in charge
told the drivers to stop work.
'If we've found a dinosaur's footprint,
we may find some more,' he said.
'We must be careful.
They are very, very rare.'

'Let's go to the museum
and tell the director,' said Simon.
'That's a good idea,' said Kate.
'Yes, bring him here quickly,'
said the man in charge.

The children went off to the museum.
When they got there,
they saw a worker.
They asked to see the director.
'Can we see him soon?' asked Kate.
'We have found a dinosaur's footprint.'

The museum director saw them at once.
'Are you sure it's a dinosaur's footprint?' he asked.
'Yes, we are quite sure,' said Kate.
'We must drive there in my car,' he said.
'There's not a moment to lose.'

They drove back as fast as they could.
All the yellow machines were still.
The drivers were standing near the rock.
They were staring at the footprint.

The museum director looked
at the footprint.
'You are right!' he said.
'It is the footprint of a dinosaur.
It was made by a dinosaur
called Megalosaurus.'

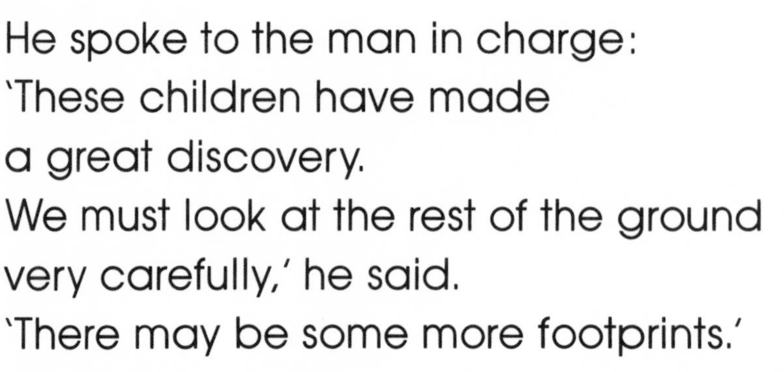

He spoke to the man in charge:
'These children have made
a great discovery.
We must look at the rest of the ground
very carefully,' he said.
'There may be some more footprints.'

'The animal that made this,'
he told them,
'was nearly twenty feet long,
and ten feet tall.
I hope we shall find
some more marks.'

The men dug very carefully with spades.
They found another mark, and another!
'You are very clever children!'
said the museum director.
'They should have their pictures
in the newspaper,'
said the man in charge.

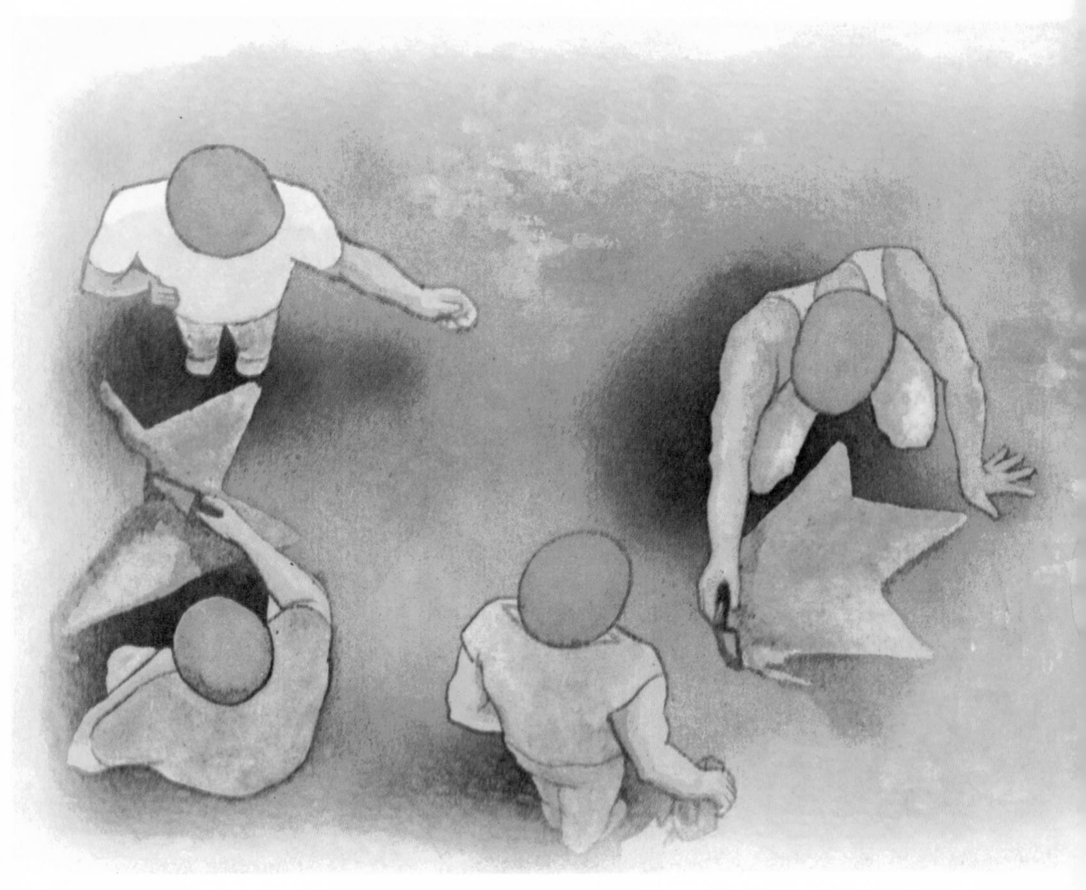

'It was Kate who found it,' said Simon.
'But it was Simon's idea to tell
the museum director,' said Kate.

'I'll take a picture of you now,'
said the museum director.
He took out his camera.
He photographed Kate and Simon
standing inside one of the footprints!
The picture was in all the newspapers.

'We only came to see
the yellow monsters,' said Simon.
'And we found a real one!' said Kate.
She looked around her,
at the marks made
by the big yellow machines.

'Do you think,' said Kate,
'that, millions of years from now,
someone will find
the wheel-marks and tracks
of our big yellow monsters?'
'It would be exciting if they did!'
said Simon.

Each information book is linked to a story in the new **Starters** program. Both kinds of book are graded into progressive reading levels – red, blue, and green. Titles in the program include:

Starters Facts	**Starters Stories**
RED 1: Going to the Zoo	RED 1: Zoo for Sale
RED 2: Birds	RED 2: The Birds from Africa
RED 3: Clowns	RED 3: Sultan's Elephants
RED 4: Going to the Hospital	RED 4: Rosie's Hospital Story
RED 5: Going to School	RED 5: Danny's Class
BLUE 1: Space Travel	BLUE 1: The Space Monster
BLUE 2: Cars	BLUE 2: The Red Racing Car
BLUE 3: Dinosaurs	BLUE 3: The Dinosaur's Footprint
BLUE 4: Christmas	BLUE 4: Palace of Snow
BLUE 5: Trains	BLUE 5: Mountain Express
GREEN 1: Airport	GREEN 1: Flight into Danger
GREEN 2: Moon	GREEN 2: Anna and the Moon Queen
GREEN 3: Forts and Castles	GREEN 3: The Secret Castle
GREEN 4: Stars	GREEN 4: The Lost Starship
GREEN 5: Earth	GREEN 5: Nuka's Tale

First published 1980 by
Macdonald Educational Ltd.,
Holywell House,
Worship Street,
London EC2

ISBN 0-382-06503-4
Published in the United States by
Silver Burdett Company
Morristown, New Jersey
1980 Printing

Library of Congress
Catalog Card No. 80-52533

Editor: Annabel McLaren
Teacher Panel: Susan Alston, Susan Batten, Ann Merriman, Julia Rickell, Gwen Trier
Subject Consultant: Dr. Alan Charig
Production: Rosemary Bishop